Dax to the Max: Blah Bla an enchanting and empov the reader on a journey with a young boy learning to overcome his fears. With imaginative storytelling, Dax battles his "stinky blobs" of negative self-talk and discovers his inner superpower. This delightful tale entertains and imparts valuable lessons on self-belief and the power of positive thinking, making it a must-read for children and parents alike.

— **Dr. Joanette,** International Best-Selling Author of Children's Books

In *Dax to the Max: Blah Blah Blobs Vs Power Pods*, the author crafts an engaging and empowering story for young readers. The book follows Dax, a relatable and endearing character who struggles with self-doubt and insecurity on the playground and beyond. These challenging feelings take center stage until the night Dax encounters MAX, a pint-sized, confident version of himself who lives in his mind.

— **Sherry Dunn,** International Best Seller and Mom's Choice Award Winner

Scott Feld's *Dax to the MAX* is a delightful blend of adventure, humor, and heart that teaches kids an invaluable lesson: the power of believing in yourself. Through Dax's exciting encounters with the Blobs and his lovable guide Max, young readers learn that courage isn't the absence of fear but the will to overcome it. This book is a wonderful reminder for children everywhere that with a little practice and positivity, they can accomplish amazing things.

— **Judy O'Beirn,** Founder and President of Hasmark Publishing International

Published by
Hasmark Publishing International
www.hasmarkpublishing.com

Copyright © 2024 Scott Feld

First Edition

No part of this book may be reproduced or transmitted in any form or by any means, electronic or mechanical, including photocopying, recording or by any information storage and retrieval system, without written permission from the author, except for the inclusion of brief quotations in a review.

Disclaimer:
This book is designed to provide information and motivation to our readers. It is sold with the understanding that the publisher is not engaged to render any type of psychological, legal, or any other kind of professional advice. The content of each article is the sole expression and opinion of its author, and not necessarily that of the publisher. No warranties or guarantees are expressed or implied by the publisher's choice to include any of the content in this volume. Neither the publisher nor the individual author(s) shall be liable for any physical, psychological, emotional, financial, or commercial damages, including, but not limited to, special, incidental, consequential or other damages. Our views and rights are the same: You are responsible for your own choices, actions, and results.

Permission requests should be addressed in writing to
Scott Feld at Scott.Feld@mindzenmotion.com.

Editors: Jeff Charles (Jeff.Charles@mindzenmotion.com) and
       Stacey Kartagener (Stacey.Kartagener@mindzenmotion.com)

Cover Design: Anne Karklins (anne@hasmarkpublishing.com)

Illustrator: Kezzia Crossley (info@kezziacrossley.com)

Interior Layout: Amit Dey (amit@hasmarkpublishing.com)

ISBN 13: 978-1-77482-210-4
ISBN 10: 1-77482-210-5

DEDICATION

To Dax, my 8-year-old son who allows me to show him his own I.S.P and makes me proud every day. I love you buddy.

To my wife Darcy who supports and encourages me to follow my dreams.

To my friends and business partners, Jeff and Stacey, thank you for always having my back, no matter how wild or quirky my ideas may be.

ACKNOWLEDGEMENTS

To all the amazing parents and kids! Thanks for jumping into this adventure with Dax, and MAX. You're now part of a "Power Team" ready to take on whatever comes your way. By diving into these pages, you too will find your own Inner Super Powers (ISP)! Keep exploring, keep believing, and most importantly, keep having fun. Here's to facing every challenge, achieving all your goals, and realizing all your dreams. Go out and show the world that nothing can hold you back. You've got this— and remember, the twists and turns along the way are all just part of the adventure! Let's Go!

CHAPTER 1
Restless

"**Here we go again!**" A frustrated Dax thinks aloud while lying in his bed, staring at the ceiling, after another not-so-fun day at school, where fear got the best of him. He can't sleep. He can't stop wondering why all the other kids in the <u>world</u> never seem to be afraid to try what he thinks are "hard things," which, lately, have been almost everything. It's a BIG problem!

Something has gotten in the way of all his fun! "That's for sure." He knows it. He can feel it. But what is it and what can he do about it? These are the questions with no answers keeping him awake tonight. Lots of nights.

While overthinking, tossing and turning, flipping and flopping, desperately trying to get comfortable so he can finally fall asleep and not have to worry about anything anymore, it gets worse. Way worse!

With all of that moving about and thrashing around, Dax's legs have now become entangled in his sheets and blankets. A new problem. "Great! Awesome!"

"What do I do?" he wonders, panicking a little bit. "It kind of feels like some sort of monster has grabbed me," he imagines. "Hey, that's kind of like how it feels when I'm afraid to do something, like a monster has grabbed me. Hmm…interesting."

After assessing his situation and realizing that, if he's ever going to fall asleep, he must free himself from the cover-monster's grasp as fast as he can, he goes to work, kicking and tugging at the sheets and blankets. The monster fights back, trying to hold onto him as tight as it can. It's a fierce battle, but ultimately, Dax wins, and the covers lie powerless, tossed to the side, half on the bed and half on the floor. Dax feels pretty good about himself at the moment.

If only he had that kind of feeling of power everywhere else, maybe things would be different for him. Maybe he wouldn't feel so afraid. Maybe… That would be amazing!

Dax pulls the blankets back up and over him, making friends once again and promising not to fight. He knows he needs them for sleep tonight.

Finally, it is time! Exhausted, he closes his eyes, allowing for his mind to slow down just enough to give him a chance to dream.

CHAPTER 2
Dream Blobs

It came out of nowhere. A massive purple Blob with one giant eye and long wiggly arms grabbing at Dax, trying to pull him down into a stinky pit where other Blobs are waiting for him: Orange, Green, Yellow, Striped…

What do they all want? What is going on?

"Let go of me! I don't want to go with you!" Dax screams. The Blobs aren't listening; they don't care. They have one goal, one mission: Get Dax!

"Oh no!" he thinks to himself, as a surge of panic rushes through his body. Dax wiggles and squirms, trying his best to escape the slimy Blobs' grasp, but it's no use. The Big, Bad Blobs got him.

"Help! Leave me alone!" Dax pleads, hoping for one last chance, but it's not to be. No way, not today. The horrible Blobs are not willing to let go. Instead, they pull and yank on him with more and more force. It really feels like a hopeless situation.

Luckily, right when Dax is about to give up and give in to the mean old Blobs' relentless demands and let them take him down into their disgusting pit of doom...

He wakes up, heart racing, pulse thumping, eyes wide open, and legs all tangled in the sheets again. Dax looks around. Phew...he's in his room; it was just a dream, a nightmare really. After assuring himself he is safe, he breathes a sigh of relief.

"What was that all about?" he wonders. "Oh wait, I think I know...school yesterday!"

CHAPTER 3
Blobs at School (Yesterday)

On the playground, with all his friends around, Dax is feeling insecure and afraid. He has been feeling this way a lot lately. These feelings seem to come and go. Sometimes the fear shows up in class when the teacher asks a question, and he isn't sure he knows the answer. He is afraid he might be laughed at. Sometimes, the fear comes around when the other kids are playing soccer or baseball, and he decides not to join in, worried he will strike out or miss scoring "the BIG goal".

There is more stuff Dax is afraid of too, like being alone, trying new things, missing out, losing, falling, failing…. This is what has been keeping him up at night and giving him bad dreams when he does finally fall asleep. Dax never really knows when the fear will rear its ugly head, in the form of a Blob, and stop him from doing what he wants to do. It's very frustrating, and he has no idea what to do about it.

Today, he's checking out the monkey bars. They look, to Dax, like they are a hundred feet high and impossible to cross. He wants to conquer them, he really does, but he doesn't think he can do it. He can't seem to get up enough courage to try. When Dax thinks this way, he makes Blobs. Blobs like the ones he dreams about, and those Big Bad Blobs are always ready to stop him before he can do the things he wants to do.

His friends look like they are having so much fun. "I don't think they see Blobs," Dax says, a bit confused. "I guess these imaginary creatures, which seem so real, are only here to stop **me** from having fun," he decides. "What a bummer!"

CHAPTER 4
Sasha to the Rescue

"Go for it, Dax! You CAN do it!" While standing in front of, staring at, and worrying about the monkey bars, Dax hears his bubbly friend Sasha's encouraging words from behind him. She is always there to make Dax feel like he can do anything. Unfortunately, Dax rarely feels the same about himself. He looks up, half-smiling at her before dropping his head back down again.

The other kids, who are waiting their turn, now speak up too: "Do it, Dax!" "C'mon, Dax!" They are cheering for him, but it sounds more like peer pressure, and that pressure makes the Blobs grow bigger.

"Aha, I bet my friends and the Blobs are in on this together, trying to make my life miserable," he imagines. Dax panics. The more he thinks about it, the worse it gets, and the worse it gets, the worse he feels. The Blobs have completely taken over now.

"This is bad!" "This is horrible!" "They got me!" he screams to himself. Sasha snaps him out of his negative thinking.

"Dax, watch! I'LL go first, then you can follow me," she says as she jumps up, grabs the first bar, and speeds across, finishing with a little twirl and a smile for her friend at the end.

"Hmm, nothing bad happened to her, no Blobs when she went across the bars. Why?" Dax wonders, half-smiling back. Then he remembers, "Oh yeah, the Blobs only bother me. That's so unfair." Dax frowns.

"See? Easy. Now, it's your turn," Sasha interrupts, trying to motivate him to "go for it".

"Yikes, no way," is his immediate answer. "I don't think so. Maybe I'll do it tomorrow," he mumbles, making sure no one can hear him, thinking *he probably won't do it tomorrow.* Boom...a Blob! "Ugh!" He steps down, head down, wishing those ugly Blobs would just disappear, but they never do.

"How about soccer or baseball?" Sasha suggests, pointing to the field nearby, where other kids are playing. Dax looks around. There are now Blobs everywhere. Geez! Feeling more nervous than ever, he shakes his head "no" to Sasha's offer.

"It's okay, Dax," she replies sweetly. "Sometimes I feel scared too," she admits. "You know I'm afraid of spiders and snakes, and I've never been able to get myself to swim across the pool in the deep end or jump off the diving board, so you are definitely not alone." "Hmm, does this mean Sasha sees Blobs too?" Dax wonders. "Oh, and I've seen you do lots of things other kids can't do too," she continues. Dax can't think of anything he does that others can't do. He feels Sasha is just being nice, but he's not going to argue with her. It's good to hear, even if it's probably not true. "Sasha is a great friend." Dax thinks to himself and smiles.

"Hey, let's go play in the sand instead, *again,* if you want." Sasha interrupts Dax's thought. "Okay." Dax nods. That is his "safe place." He doesn't ever remember seeing any Blobs while playing in the sand, and so, off they go.

CHAPTER 5

Funzi

A couple more tough days and restless nights later, at bedtime, Dax's dad, who likes to call himself "Funzi" because of his job as a toy inventor and his always positive attitude, is ready for their usual nighttime routine. After pajamas and teeth brushing, and before book reading, Funzi puts on music and shows Dax one of the toys or games he is currently working on.

Dax usually gives him a thumbs-up, thumbs-down, or thumbs-sideways, depending on how he feels about his dad's latest creation and presentation. Then they laugh, sing, and dance until one or both fall into bed exhausted. Funzi starts the show. "And this is my newest invention… da-ta-da… I call it: 'The Hand Hoop.' Isn't it amazing?" he asks enthusiastically while spinning it wildly.

"Sure, Dad," Dax answers, seemingly disinterested. Funzi stops what he's doing and looks at Dax, concerned. "What's up, son? Something wrong? Want to talk about it?"

"No, not really, unless you can say something that will make me feel braver," Dax answers hopefully.

His dad thinks for a moment, then says, "Braver, huh? What's going on?"

"Nothing, never mind," Dax reacts, looking away, then quickly turning back to his dad, now speaking fast and loud, surprising himself: "I just can't do what the other kids can do. I'm always afraid I'm going to fall, or get hurt, or everyone will laugh at me, or something bad will happen. I don't even know why." Dax drops his head into his pillow, feeling like he wants to cry. He had been holding that in for a long time.

"Oh no, I know how THAT goes," says Funzi with a gentle nod.

"Really?" This surprises Dax. He sits up. "You feel afraid too? What do you do about it?" he asks enthusiastically.

"Well, let me tell you." Funzi puts his hand hoop to the side for the moment to help his son. "When I was about your age, my dad and my mom, your grandpa and grandma, told me an amazing secret. They said—ready for it?" Dax nods. "Okay… Drum roll, guitar, flute, trombone, violin…" Funzi acts out every instrument.

"Okay, okay, come on, Dad! Just tell me already PLEASE!" Dax really wants to know.

"Right, the secret… Here it is… As it turns out, we ALL have…" Funzi is about to speak when…

CHAPTER 6
Kobe Kangaroo

A friendly kangaroo pokes his head into Dax's room, his ears twitching with curiosity. "Hey, Kobe!" Dax greets him excitedly. Kobe Kangaroo comes hopping in. "Hi, Mom, I can see you too," Dax says with a smile.

Dax's mom enters behind Kobe with her hand attached to the little stuffed animal hand puppet. She's always pretending Kobe is real, which never fails to make Dax burst into laughter.

Kobe isn't just any toy; he's Dax's favorite prop, which his mom uses when she teaches drama at the local theater. She finds speaking through Kobe Kangaroo helps her connect better with her son. Dax's mom likes to remind him that a kangaroo is a very special animal.

"A kangaroo is energetic, provides security with its pouch, and can also teach us about courage," she says proudly. "The name Kobe means 'little forest,' which can bring about a feeling of tranquility and calmness." Dax loves to hear about Kobe Kangaroo. He always feels a lot better when Kobe is around.

Mom, using Kobe to talk, asks, "Whatcha all doing in here? Guy stuff?"

"No, no, no...I was just about to tell Dax 'The BIG Secret,'" Funzi responds with a wink.

"What 'BIG Secret' is that?" Mom questions in her own voice.

"The one about Inner Super Powers—you know, those powers we all have inside of us. The ones that make us TOUGHER than our FEARS," Funzi says loudly, flexing his muscles. Dax looks confused but he is listening.

"Oh yes! That BIG Secret," Mom confirms. Then, back to using Kobe to speak for her, says, "Fear can keep us from doing what we want to do. Boo-Hoo." Kobe Kangaroo pretends to cry, trying to make Dax smile. It works. Kobe always seems to "get" how Dax is feeling. "Now, what are you afraid of, little Joey?" (her nickname for Dax when using Kobe to talk to him).

"Everything!" Dax says abruptly while yawning. It's been quite a day for Dax, and he hasn't slept that well lately with all those pesky Blobs trying to get him. Kobe can see Dax is getting tired. Mom and Dad see it too. "We'll talk more about this in the morning," Funzi assures his son.

"Until then, I hope you have Super Dreams," Dax's mom adds in her own sweet voice, giving him a gentle kiss goodnight.

"I think he just might," whispers Funzi with a knowing smile as they turn out the lights and exit the room.

CHAPTER 7
Meet MAX

"Dax, Dax, DAX!"

"What? What? What do you want?" Dax responds sleepily, covering his head with his pillow. "Who's there?" he asks, not recognizing the voice.

"Dax, Dax, DAX!" he hears the voice again.

"What is going on?" he wonders, feeling slightly annoyed. Who would dare wake him up in the middle of the night?

Much to his surprise, when he moves the pillow and opens his eyes, he finds a very strange sight: Floating above his head, dressed in a superhero outfit, complete with cape and mask, with the letters "MAX" written across his chest, is a mini version of himself looking a bit irritated. His hands are on his hips, and there is a pouty look on his face.

"AAH! Who Are YOU?" Dax screams. "Where did you come from? What are you doing here?"

"Who? Where? What? All great questions," is the calm response.

"Are there some great answers?" Dax asks hopefully.

"There sure are!" the mini superhero exclaims. And so, a new adventure begins...

CHAPTER 8
Dax and MAX

"Let's start with the 'Who?' I am MAX. Capital 'M', capital 'A', capital 'X'," he proudly states, pointing to his chest. "I am YOU, to the MAX-imum. You know, YOU...at your very BEST!" "Huh?" Dax is confused. MAX continues, "Now, the 'Where.' That is a bit more complicated, and I think it's best I show you. Let's go for a ride. What do you say?"

Before Dax can answer, MAX wraps his cape around him and off they go.

And, what a ride it is! Dax holds on tight. "Where are you taking me?" he asks nervously.

MAX smiles widely. "You asked where I came from, so I'm taking you **there**."

"But where is **there**, MAX?"

"**There** is usually my favorite place to be, but not lately. It's the place where you will get to see and use your own I.S.P., eventually and hopefully," MAX responds, crossing his fingers. This sounds like some sort of riddle to Dax.

"What are you talking about? What is I.S.P.?" Dax asks, feeling very unsure about all this. "It sounds scary!"

"Scary? No, no, no! Your I.S.P. is good, it will set you free from your wor-eee. Truuuuust me!" MAX answers, his voice trailing off as he zooms faster through the air.

Dax holds on even tighter, as tightly as he can. "But what does I.S.P. mean?" he questions.

"I.S.P.? Oh, that's easy: Inner Super Powers, of course," MAX says with a wink.

"Inner Super Powers? Cool!"

('Wait….,' Dax thinks for a moment. Where had he heard that before?)

Psst…His dad (Funzi) said it, remember?

CHAPTER 9
Stink Think

"We're here," MAX announces with a drop and a sudden stop. "Look around, check it out, Dax."

The space is filled with lots of images, lights, colors, and sounds all moving around very quickly in every direction, all at the same time. It's really quite chaotic. Dax notices immediately. "This is wild, MAX! Where are we?"

"This is where I live, this is my HOME. This is your MIND. This is what it looks and feels like most of the time, lots and lots going on," MAX says casually, smiling. "I'm giving you a little glimpse inside."

"Wait, what? This is my MIND? We're in my MIND? You live in my MIND?" Dax asks, beyond confused. "MAX, WHAT ARE YOU TALKING ABOUT?"

MAX laughs a little, then replies, "Okay, I guess that is a lot to understand, but don't worry, soon it will all make perfect sense. Let's start at the beginning so I can explain why I am here."

"That would be great!" Dax says, calming himself down for the moment. He is curious to find out what's going on.

"Watch this!" MAX exclaims with a nervous grin. He flips a switch, and suddenly, all the images, lights, colors, and sounds swirl together. They merge into one brilliant, glowing sphere that explodes outward to form a giant 360° screen that flickers to life all around them. It begins playing a scene from earlier that day, a memory Dax would rather forget.

He looks up to watch, then quickly drops his head. "That was me with Sasha at school today." The screen shows the playground, the monkey bars, and the sports field where kids are playing soccer and baseball. It also shows Dax not playing, not trying, and most importantly, not thinking he can do any of it. As the memory on the screen continues replaying this unfortunate experience, a terrible smell starts to fill the space.

"Ew, what's that stink? MAX, did you just…?"

MAX laughs. "No, I did NOT just… That's not from ME. That stink…is your THINK!"

Dax coughs. He can hardly breathe. A thick multicolored haze begins to fill the air.

"MAX, make it stop," Dax pleads.

"No can do, that will be a job for you. Not just yet though. Wait for it, here it comes…Wham, Bam, Shazam! And THERE they are!" MAX points. The stinky haze has now gathered itself into gross blobby-looking creatures, like the ones he imagined on the playground and sees in his really bad dreams.

"Oh no, not again!" Dax screams, terrified!

"These guys keep showing up here acting like they own the place, and I can't take it anymore," MAX says, stomping his foot down like he's mad.

"Sorry, MAX!" Dax feels bad.

"I can't live here like this, with them," MAX continues, gesturing towards the Blobs. One of the Blobs, the purple one, whose name is Algo, Dax finds out later, sticks his tongue out at MAX. MAX shakes his head. "Something, or someTHINK, has to change, and THAT is why I am here. I need your help, Dax, to defeat them, to make them go away," MAX says, now looking extremely determined.

CHAPTER 10
Big, Bad, Blah Blah Blobs

Afraid and unsure of what is happening and how to help MAX, Dax is worried. He nervously asks, "What, what are they?"

MAX responds, "Not WHAT, but WHO are they? Those are the Big, Bad, Blah Blah Blobs. Disgusting, aren't they?"

"The purple one is Algo," MAX explains. "He seems to like to show up whenever you use 'getting hurt' as an *unreasonable* excuse for not trying. He's been around a lot lately." Dax thinks about the monkey bars and how almost everyone else at school at least tries them and no one really ever gets hurt. Hmm.

"The striped one with the three eyes is Atych. Atych is the Blob that comes from your 'fear of failure.' When you won't play soccer or baseball or try something new because you think you won't do well, Atych comes to life. He's also been here a lot lately, come to think of it," MAX says, shaking his head.

"The last one I'll introduce you to is Thasso," MAX says. "He is the green one. Although I have to admit he's kind of cute, don't let that fool you. Thasso is a tricky Blob. When you worry that nothing good will happen to you, when you think you won't be able to achieve your goals, here comes Thasso, ready to get in your way."

"There are more Blobs too, but these are the ones I've been dealing with the most lately and the ones you need to help me get rid of right now, Dax." MAX continues, now talking in a more serious tone.

"You see, these crazy creatures mostly only show up when you:

Could, but Don't believe you Can, So You Don't Do What you want to Do!

They come directly from and for YOU! Pee-Yew!" MAX states, sounding like he's talking in riddles again.

"Wait, what? Huh? I don't get it." Dax's head is spinning, the smell is getting to him, and there are Blobs right in front of him. It's all too much. "What did you say, MAX?"

"I said, you don't believe in YOU, and that is the P.U."

"Aha!" It's a lightbulb moment for Dax. It is all starting to make sense. "Like me at school today?" he questions, already knowing the answer.

MAX points at the screen again. "Yep, JUST like you at school today, yesterday, and just like you, every time you let that worried, fear-filled voice inside, STOP you."

Dax nods. He gets it. They both hold their noses and exchange a knowing smile. "What can I do, MAX?" Dax asks, not sure he wants to hear the answer. "Ah, I'm glad you asked," MAX replies. "I'll show you." And with that, MAX flips another switch, and when he does, they are suddenly in the most beautiful space Dax has ever seen. It feels so right, so perfect.

CHAPTER 11

Power-UP

"Wow, MAX, this is amazing!" Dax says, staring in complete awe at everything all around him. "I know, I know," MAX nods with a big smile. "I'm glad you like it. I do too." Dax loves it. He feels both weightless and powerful at the same time. This is a very new, exciting experience for Dax.

"I'm showing you what your mind can be like when you get rid of the stink and choose to Power Think," MAX tells Dax.

"In other words, when there is Positivity, this, right here, right now, is what you will feel and see. This is how it's supposed to be, Blob-free.

This is where dreams come true for me and for you. This represents a different and better way to experience life. It is filled with warmth and light, hope, joy, and happiness. Do you see it? Do you feel it, Dax?" MAX asks with a peaceful smile.

"I do see it, I do feel it," Dax confirms with an enthusiastic nod.

"When you operate from here, anything and everything is possible, Dax." As MAX speaks, he starts to glow. "MAX, what's happening to you?" Dax asks. "Oh, that's the inner power I feel when I get to hang out here." MAX smiles but then his face turns serious again. "You need to know, Dax, I can only show you this amazing space, and let you feel it briefly, but to make it real, and make it last, I need your help. We have to do this together." As MAX shares, the "Power Place" and his glow start to fade away. Dax doesn't want it to go. He loves it here! He feels so good here, like he can do anything here. "This is where I always want to be, MAX." MAX nods. "Me too, Dax, me too!" "So what do I need to do? Please tell me," Dax pleads with a new sense of urgency.

"You must learn to Power Think," MAX responds. "We have to build up your Inner Super Powers, your I.S.P. And Power Thinking is the key."

"Okay, MAX, I want to help. I want to Power Think. How do I learn to do it?" Dax inquires, very excited to be part of 'a Power Team' for once.

"You Prax, Dax, of course. Prax is the only way to build a super strong I.S.P. A super strong ME. Then we'll get to stay here, like this, Blob-free. Yip-ee!" MAX does a little dance. "What do you think, Dax?"

Dax thinks MAX is speaking in riddles again. "Prax? What is Prax, MAX?" Dax asks.

"Oh, Prax, you know, Practice," MAX responds, like that was so obvious. "Right, Prax. Okay, I can Prax, MAX," Dax says, smiling. He kind of likes learning this new, mini superhero lingo.

"So...what do I Prax so I can Power Think, MAX?" "Great question, Dax." MAX is excited to share so they can finally defeat those annoying Blobs together.

"First, you'll need to Prax saying to yourself what you DO want to hear. You know, really positive self-talk," MAX begins.

Then, you'll need to Prax seeing yourself DOING what you WANT to do, even if you feel scared," MAX says with a thumbs up.

"Okay, MAX, I'll Prax," Dax promises. He's hesitant as usual, but this time, willing to try.

"Great. Cool. Awesome...let's begin," MAX celebrates.

"First, we have to go back and have a quick look at some of your latest fears," MAX states.

"Wait, why do we have to do that?" Dax wonders, not really liking where this is going. "Maybe I don't want to Prax after all," Dax exclaims nervously.

"You have to face your fear to make it disappear," MAX says, smiling, proud of his latest rhyme. Let's just do it! Okay?" Dax shrugs. MAX flips his magic switch, and just like that, there is an image on the screen of a bunch of kids playing soccer. "Would you go play with them?" MAX boldly asks. Dax thinks for a second, then replies, "Uhm, NO. MAX! There is no way. I mean, it looks like it could be fun, but I don't think they'd want me to play. I'm not very good at soccer."

MAX nods, flipping the screen to a baseball game. "How about baseball?" he inquires.

"No, no thanks…I'm even worse at baseball," Dax responds, shaking his head sadly. MAX can see why Blobs are always hanging around in Dax's mind.

Another flip of the switch and an image of Dax at school shows up. The teacher is asking for a volunteer to do a math problem in front of the class. "Would you raise your hand?" MAX asks. Dax responds, as MAX expected, "No way, Jose!"

"I see. Let's look at one more scene." MAX flips the screen one last time, now showing an image of a playground with monkey bars and other equipment to climb on, under, over, and around. "Would you go play on any of that?" MAX asks Dax, pointing to the screen. "Hmm, maybe, I don't know. It looks kind of hard. I might fall. I might not make it. I don't want to risk it. I don't think I would try," Dax says, hanging his head.

"What's wrong with me?" he wonders aloud, not really expecting an answer.

"Nothing is wrong with you, Dax," MAX assures him while holding his nose again, pointing to the Blobs who have reappeared. "You just need to learn to Power Think so there is less Stink," MAX tells Dax with a nod and a smile.

"Wait, the Blobs are back?" Dax asks, surprised and worried.

"You brought them here," MAX tells Dax. "You thought you couldn't, you thought you might not do well, be bad at, fall, fail… You did it! Blobs come from Stink Think, and, right now, as we faced your fears, your Thinkin' was a Stinkin'. But don't worry, now that we have the Blobs here, let's Power-UP and take them down together, as a team! Let's Prax, Dax!" MAX is fired up.

CHAPTER 12
Power Thinking

MAX turns to Dax with a thoughtful expression, his voice changing to a soft yet serious tone. "Dax, you asked what I am doing here? Why I came? Remember?"

"Yeah, yeah, I remember," Dax responds.

"Well, now you know. I came to help you STOP your Stink Think and START to Power Think, because when you Power Think, the Blobs will shrink. And, when they shrink, YOU are in control and get to do what YOU want to do. No Blob will ever STOP you! You get it, you got it, Dax? Do you understand, rubber-band? Are you picking up what I'm putting down? Is it clear? We have to get Power over the Fear," MAX raps. He is on a roll. "If you are ready, I can show you how, right now!" MAX tells Dax hopefully.

Dax smiles and nods. "I am ready! Let's do this!"

"Great, good, okay. The first step is super-duper easy. Just repeat after me," MAX tells Dax. "Say, 'I can, I will! I can, I will,' over and over and over and over and over and over and over again, while thinking about **what you DO want to do.**"

"That's it?" Dax wonders, surprised. It doesn't seem too hard, so he does what he is told, but strangely, it comes out softly, more like a question than a statement. "I can? I will?" Hmm, not so easy after all. MAX shakes his head. "Louder! Like this." He demonstrates: "I can! I will! I can! I will! I CAN! I WILL! Say it like you MEAN it and like you really BELIEVE it!" MAX is pumped! But the Blobs look like they are laughing at him. They don't seem worried at all.

Dax tries again, this time with a little more "oomph," and as he does, a slight bright light begins to glow, then it fades away. "What was that?" Dax asks.

CHAPTER 13

PowerPods

"That was YOU! Woo-Hoo! You created a little mini-PowerPod with your positive Power Thoughts," MAX states proudly. "Just like you can make a Blob with your Stink Think, you can make a PowerPod with your Power Think. That's the 'Glow Bro!'" MAX tells Dax as Dax laughs at MAX's "cool talk". "It was nowhere near big enough to defeat a Blob YET, but it sure is a great start. I'm proud of you," MAX says, putting his mini arm on Dax's shoulder. Dax is starting to feel really good about himself for the first time in a long time, and the Blobs, for the first time in a long time, look a little bit nervous.

"You did great! You just need more Prax," MAX tells Dax. "Hey, I think you're ready for the next level of I.S.P., so come with me!" MAX grabs Dax and off they fly, way up high into the sky. "Wee!"

CHAPTER 14
Visualize

MAX suddenly stops midair and asks Dax, "Would you like to know more about how to be Tougher than your Fears so you can play games, swing on monkey bars, not feel left out, and do all the fun stuff you want to do?" The Blobs are watching from down below with interest.

"Tougher than my Fears?" *Dax has heard this somewhere before too.

It was Funzi! Funzi said it, remember?

"Yes, please! Of course! That's ALL I want!" Dax responds, now very excited.

"Okay, listen closely," MAX says, moving in like he's about to share a BIG secret. "The next trick, to go from Stink to Power Think, is to close your eyes and visualize."

"Visu-a-what?" Dax asks.

"Visualize. It's easy. Imagine yourself doing IT! See yourself climbing, laughing, playing, and having fun in whatever IT is you want to do, before you actually DO IT."

"If you're able to see it up here," MAX points to Dax's head, "...you'll be able to do it out there—on the playground, on the field, in the classroom, anywhere and everywhere you want. You'll be Un-Stoppable, Dax. Are you ready to 'Go for it?'" he asks, sounding extremely excited to keep moving forward.

Dax likes what he hears. Un-Stoppable sounds amazing, but he is hesitant. "Honestly, it sounds kind of weird, MAX. See it up here?" Dax questions, pointing to his own head. "Do it out there? I don't know, I guess I'll give it a try. I really do want to be 'Tougher than my Fears!' I really do want to get back to that 'Power Place.'" He remembers how good he felt there.

"Okay, MAX, let's do it." Dax closes his eyes to try and visualize. Almost immediately, he opens his eyes. "I don't see it. I can't do it. It's too hard, MAX. I can't see myself doing anything I want to do," Dax states, feeling frustrated and wanting to give up. The Blobs move in closer, growing bigger along with Dax's fears, doubts, worries, and negative thoughts.

MAX encourages Dax to push on. "Don't give up! Don't let the Blobs win! Remember, it just takes some Prax, Dax. You CAN definitely do it!"

Dax hears MAX and he knows he is right. He closes his eyes and tries again and again, and again, and again to visualize…he keeps trying and trying and trying. He tries to see himself scoring a goal, or getting a hit, being the first to raise his hand in class and, of course, he tries to visualize crossing those "impossible" monkey bars. He tries to see himself doing all sorts of things but…no luck until, finally…something changes. "What's this?" Something clicks. "What's happening?" The screen flickers…

"Wait, I think I got it, MAX!" Dax exclaims, closing his eyes tighter. "I think it's working! I'm doing it, I can see myself kicking a ball into a goal." That was cool! Dax shouts, "GOOOOOAAAAL!" just like he had seen on TV.

"Okay, baseball... I see myself, I'm up to bat. I swing, I get a hit. It's a big one. It's a home run. I'm rounding the bases, and everyone is cheering. Yea! This is the BEST!" Dax is so excited!

"Time for class. I'm at my desk. The teacher asks a question: 'What's the capital of the United States?' I know it, I think I know it. No, I definitely know it. I raise my hand, I feel butterflies in my stomach, and the teacher calls on me...'Washington, D.C.,'" I answer.

"Correct, Dax," the teacher says, smiling.

"I realize in that moment, I usually answer correctly, in my head, but this is the first time I've seen myself get up the nerve to answer in front of my whole class. It feels pretty great," Dax admits.

Finally, still visualizing, Dax moves onto the monkey bars. He sees himself "Going for It." He takes a deep breath, and in his mind, which is becoming more and more powerful, he reaches out and grabs the first bar. Then he swings to the second, the third, the fourth, fifth, sixth, and all the way to the end with a big Ta-Da! "Wow! This visualizing is so cool!" exclaims Dax, opening his eyes to MAX clapping for him with a big smile on his little superhero face.

"Dax, that was amazing! You are doing great! There is just one more thing I want you to Prax just to make

sure you are fully 'inner super-powered' to defeat any and all Blobs that ever try to get in your way," MAX states, once again, in a more serious tone, letting Dax know this is important.

"What is it, MAX?" Dax hopes he can do what MAX is about to ask of him.

"I want you to visualize again, but this time, I want you to see yourself NOT succeeding so easily," MAX says sincerely. Dax thinks he must be joking. After all this teaching and training to Power him UP, MAX could not actually be asking him to purposely see himself falling or failing, the things he fears the most!

"MAX, wait, what? If this is a joke, I don't get it," Dax says, feeling confused.

"No joke," MAX says, quite seriously. "Let me explain."

"Yes, please." Dax is eager to hear how visualizing *not succeeding* could be helpful in any way.

MAX tells Dax, "You must be able to Power Think even when it doesn't work out, you don't make it, you don't win...because that's real life, my friend. Being able to Power Think no matter what the result is, well that is the true I.S.P. that can and will set you free." As MAX talks, he is starting to glow again. Dax can feel how important this step is in getting back to that amazing, incredible Power Place he loves so much. "Let's do it, MAX," Dax states. He is ready to go.

"Okay, Dax, I want you to Power Think while you Visualize, so you can Prax being tougher than your fears when you face them head-on," MAX explains. Dax considers this for a moment, then asks, "Are you saying not to Stink Think and make Blobs if I fail? If I don't get a hit, or score a goal? If I don't get the answer right, or I don't make it across the monkey bars?

Is that right, MAX?"

"Yes, that's exactly right, Dax. If you don't succeed, try, try again, and in order to try, try again, you must stay Powered-Up no matter what. You can say something like, "I can, I will, *try again"* when it doesn't quite work out the way you hoped. "How's that sound, Dax?"

"That sounds good to me, MAX. Really good, actually! I'm ready!" Dax says, closing his eyes to once again visualize. He chooses the monkey bars because that's what made the most Blobs appear the other day at school. "Okay, here I go." He closes his eyes. He sees himself reaching out, grabbing the first bar. "I got it." Good. Now, the second. "Got it, too. I'm holding on tight, swinging out for the third bar, and then...I see myself slipping off and falling down to the ground."

"Okay, Dax," MAX joins in.

"Now, as your feet hit the ground, notice you didn't get hurt, nobody is laughing, and you actually feel really good that you tried. Go ahead, do it again, see yourself getting further and further every time until you make it all the way across." Dax does exactly what he is told.

"Finally, Dax, before you open your eyes, realize it was all progress, all the time," MAX tells him. "Even when you didn't make it, you got better and better with each attempt. It's the same in everything you do but, if you never actually *do*, that's when there is the P.U."

"Ew, yuck," they both say at the same time, laughing. "Okay, Dax, open your eyes. There's a BIG surprise."

CHAPTER 15
The Cape

A big ball of bright light is now glowing all around them. "Look, MAX! Is this Power Pod big enough to defeat the Big Bad Blah Blah Blobs?" Dax asks. He is so excited, and so is MAX!

"It sure looks like it," MAX exclaims proudly, "but there's only one way to find out for sure. Quick, grab a piece off the Pod and throw it at those stinky Blobs," MAX instructs, flying them lower and closer to their target. The Blobs are now looking quite worried and quite scared.

"Just throw?" Dax confirms, wanting to be sure.

"Yep, throw, throw, throw, 'throw the glow' at Thasso, Atych, and Algo. Go! Go!" As Dax does what he is told, the Blobs are hit. Suddenly, there is a "poof," a light flashes, and Wham, Bam, Shazam! The Blobs turn back into a multicolor haze which, amazingly, morphs into a multicolor cape that floats up and over to Dax, landing on his shoulders. And, with that, Dax's mind turns back to the way it's meant to be...Powered-UP and Blob-Free.

MAX, standing proud, chants:
"Dax... Dax... Dax..."

CHAPTER 16

Back Home

"Dax, Dax, Dax, wake up!" It's his dad's voice. "Do you want to go to the park with Sasha today? Her mom just called."

Still half asleep, Dax is confused. Was his adventure with MAX all just a dream?

"Um, sure, Dad, I'll go." Dax yells back down the stairs. "I'll go; Algo... Coincidence?" He shakes it off, looking around his room. It seems the same as before, but somehow, he feels very, very different. Hmm...

CHAPTER 17
On the Playground

Dax's dad (Funzi) and his mom (with Kobe, as usual) watch from the bench with Sasha's parents while Sasha and Dax run toward the playground.

"Sasha!" Dax turns to his friend. "I am going to go across the entire climbing course today. Monkey Bars, Cargo Net, Beam, the whole thing," he says confidently, surprising himself.

"Wait, what?" Sasha is unsure, remembering what happened at school, but before she can talk to him about it, Dax races up the ladder to start. Sasha is concerned for her friend. "Dax, you don't have to do this. We can just play in the sand again."

But Dax is on a mission to prove something to himself. He closes his eyes to visualize—See It! Do It! Then, he takes a deep breath and shouts those seemingly magic words that have changed everything for him: "I can! I will! I CAN! I WILL!" He decides to add "LET'S GO!" for a little extra power.

Amazingly, when he opens his eyes, he is ready. There are no Blobs in sight. As if he is still wearing his cape, he jumps up and swings from bar to bar. He's on his way until, oops, he slips. He falls down. He lands on his feet. Everyone is worried, except DAX. He jumps back up onto the ladder and starts all over again...

"I can, I will, try and try again until I make it," he declares. Then off he goes, Try #2, Try #3, Try #4, further and further each time. "Progress," he reminds himself. Dax is staying strong in his thoughts and so, on Try #5, he conquers those no longer "impossible" monkey bars, and all the other obstacles too. With a loud "Woo-Hoo," he heads down the Whirly-Twirly Slide for a big finish! He did it! Dax did it, and this time, it wasn't a dream.

CHAPTER 18
Superhero Dax

The moms, dads, Kobe, and Sasha all rush over to congratulate him.

"Wow, Dax, I thought you said yesterday you were afraid to do things like this?" Funzi questions, both surprised and proud.

Dax explains, "I was, Dad, but then I found my Inner Super Powers and became 'Tougher than my Fears,' just like you said." Everybody smiles. Sasha gives him a high-five.

Kobe, with Mom's help, pats Dax on the back. "I always knew you had it in you little Joey, and now, YOU know it too."

"You truly are amazing, son," Dax's mom says in her own voice, giving him a loving hug.

Dax looks around, thinking of MAX, Prax, Blobs, and Power Pods. "No more Stinkin' Thinkin' for me!" he declares. And with that, it's official: Dax is now Free, to See and Be, his I.S.P., and it's no longer just in his dreams. It's real and it's true. And the best part is, it's not just for Dax. It's real and true for YOU too!

THE END

Interesting Facts about the Characters in This Story:

- The name "Sasha" means "Defender/Helper."
- Kangaroo: The kangaroo's spiritual energy encourages people to seek guidance in times of need. In the kangaroo's presence, we find courage with a sense of security.
- The name "Kobe" means "Little Forest" and evokes feelings of calmness and serenity.
- The UP in Power UP = Unlimited Possibility, Power, and Potential.
- The Big Bad Blah Blah Blob is what we create with the never-ending chatter in our minds (specifically, the negative self-talk).
- "I.S.P." is for You and for ME. It stands for: "Inner Super Power," and we all have it within us!

ABOUT THE AUTHOR

Scott Feld is a proud father to his 8-year-old son, Dax, who serves as the inspiration behind *Dax to the MAX*. As a Master Certified Empowerment Coach, Scott has spent over 30 years working with children of all ages, guiding them to unlock their potential. Recognizing that many kids struggle to use their minds to their full advantage, Scott created *Dax to the MAX* as part of his broader "Power-UP Experiences" movement, empowering kids to discover and harness their Inner SuperPowers (ISP).

WANT MORE DAX to the MAX?

Scan the QR Code

https://scottfeld.com

OTHER BOOKS AVAILABLE

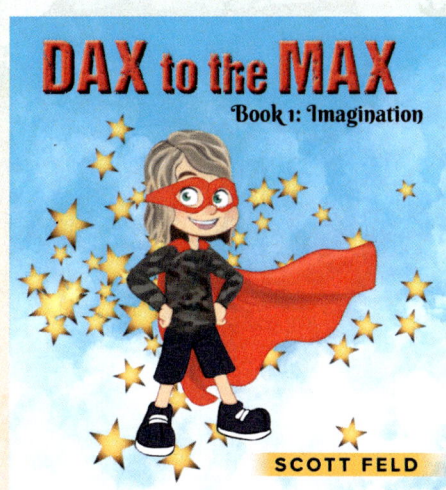

Dax to the Max
Book 1: Imagination

Dax to the Max
Activity Book

These books aim to nurture the hidden SuperPower of Imagination that young children have often not learned to tap, and to make them aware that anything is possible when we add intention to our thinking.

Available on Amazon

Made in the USA
Middletown, DE
25 January 2025

70095152R00042